NORTON'S FIRST SHOW

by Bernadette Kelly

illustrated by Liz Alger

capstone

Published in the United States in 2010, 2014
by Picture Window Books, a Capstone Imprint
1710 Roe Crest Drive
North Mankato, Minnesota 56003
www.capstonepub.com

First published as *Norton's Blue Ribbon*
in Australia in 2008 by Black Dog Books

Published by arrangement with
Walker Books Australia Pty Ltd,
Level 2, 1-15 Wilson Street,
Newtown 2042, Australia

Library of Congress Cataloging-in-Publication Data is available
on the Library of Congress website.
ISBN: 978-1-4048-5506-9 (library binding)
ISBN: 978-1-4795-2068-8 (paperback)

Summary: Oblivious to her pony's misbehaving ways, Molly enters her
beloved Norton in the horse show.

Cover design by Veronica Scott

Printed in China by Nordica
0413/CA21300496
032013   007226NORDF13

· TABLE OF CONTENTS ·

Meet Your Pony Pals

NORTON AND MOLLY

MOM

THE JUDGE

JILLIAN JONES

CHAPTER 1

SHOW PONY

Today was a big day. It was show day. It was Norton's first show day. Norton was a blue-ribbon show horse. And today the whole world would know it.

I had spent the day before getting Norton ready. I had to wash him twice. After the first wash, Norton rolled in the mud. He didn't understand that he needed to stay clean.

It was a long drive to the show. When we got there, Norton couldn't wait to get out of the trailer.

I could tell how much he was looking forward to his big day.

The cake-decorating ladies were nice.
They ran after us just to wish Norton
luck.

The people in the dog area weren't very nice. I guess they were too busy trying to keep their playful animals under control.

The man running the rides was also
a little grumpy. He probably has to deal
with crabby people all day.

We arrived at the chicken area just in time for judging. The chickens were being bad. Luckily, Norton was there. He rounded them up. Then he calmed them down.

It was easy to see that the alpacas
were jealous of Norton's good looks. Still,
I thought spitting at us was going a bit
too far.

Then Mom found us. It was time to
get ready for Norton's first event.

CHAPTER 2

LOOKING GOOD

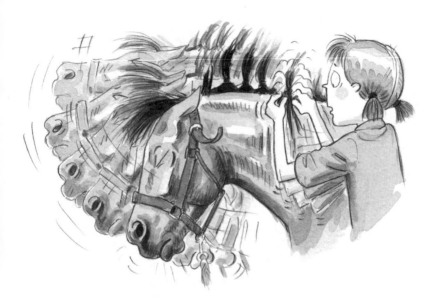

My first job was to braid Norton's mane and tail. A good pony will stand still. The braids should be evenly spaced. They are rolled into tight little balls. The final look should be neat and smooth.

"I could probably be a hairdresser when I grow up," I told Mom.

"Hmm," she said.

"Or a horse trainer," I said.

"Hmm," she said again.

Jillian Jones was having trouble getting her pony's braids right.

"Would you like some help, Jillian?" I asked. She just shook her head.

Jillian wouldn't take my advice, so
I tried to show her instead. Somehow
I messed it up. That's what you get for
trying to be nice to people.

Next I used hoof paint to make
Norton's feet look shiny. You should
always look for a flat, dirt-free area to do
this. You don't want anything sticking to
your pony's hooves.

Once Norton was groomed, it was time to saddle up.

Norton must have been hungry. He tried to take a bite out of the saddle.

"You're just going to have to wait for lunch, Norton," I told him.

CHAPTER 3

FIRST EVENT

The first event was for the best
presented horse and rider. I changed into
my show outfit. A good show rider should
be clean. It's too bad Norton needed a
hug just then.

Show outfits often have a tie. But tying a tie is not easy.

"Do you want me to help you with your tie, Jillian?" I asked.

It was lucky for Jillian that I was around. I don't know what she would do without me.

At last, Norton and I were ready to face the judge. Jillian was running late.

"Don't worry," I told her. "Not everybody's good at being organized."

Poor Jillian. She didn't stand a chance against Norton and me.

Norton knows that any last minute business should be done before entering the ring. That way there aren't any surprises.

I spotted a judge watching us. I knew she thought we were being extra polite.

The judge asked everyone to trot around in a circle. Norton wanted to show her how well he could halt. Some of the other riders forgot to smile. A good show rider will always smile, no matter what happens.

Norton likes to stand out from the crowd. We showed the judge how well we could do more than one thing at a time. Norton can actually leap sideways while trotting. He's so clever!

Norton had one last chance to show off. I'll bet none of the other ponies could wave to the crowd.

CHAPTER 4

A GOOD SPORT

A good judge will always dress up for show day. When our judge asked everybody to line up, I thought she looked very nice in her dress and hat. Norton thought so too.

The judge walked down the line of ponies. She stopped at each pony. The judge stopped for a long time in front of Jillian Jones.

It was hard for Jillian when she was up against good show riders like me. But I didn't think the judge should be too hard on Jillian. After all, everybody has to start somewhere.

I was sure that the judge had already made up her mind. But it was only right that everyone had a fair chance. The judge walked over to award Norton and me the blue ribbon for first place.

But just before she could, Norton
leaned over and ate the rose from her
hat. I don't know why she got so angry!
When horses are hungry, they eat.

The judge was so annoyed that she gave first place to Jillian Jones. We didn't even get a second or third place ribbon! I think she was still mad about the rose-eating thing.

Because I am such a good sport, I congratulated Jillian. Besides, who wanted to win the easy events? Norton and I would win the rider event.

CHAPTER 5

NAP TIME

After such an early start, Norton was tired. I let him have a short nap. After all, a good trainer knows when a horse needs to rest.

"Time to wake up, Norton. The rider event has begun," I said after an hour. "We'll have to hurry."

I knew Norton wouldn't want to miss out. The rider event was his favorite.

It is best not to make sudden movements around horses.

"Quick, Norton, the event has started," I said quietly. "If we hurry we can still make it."

Norton must have been exhausted. By the time I woke him up we had missed the event. We saw Jillian Jones ride by with another blue ribbon.

We really couldn't miss the next event.
It was for the best-behaved pony.

"Norton, you'll definitely win this
event," I told him.

It's lucky I am a fast worker. I had Norton saddled and ready to ride in a flash.

"Come on, Norton. Put your best hoof forward. Look, the judge is watching us. I think she finally noticed you!" I said proudly.

"Time to line up, Norton. Oops, careful," I said.

The ground in the ring must have been rough because Norton kept tripping. I was going to write a stern letter to the people in charge when I got home.

Suddenly there was a really loud noise overhead. A helicopter was flying right over the event ring.

"Now, Norton, stay calm," I said.

Horses are flight animals. That means they will run from danger. A good trainer can teach a horse to ignore the instinct to run. The horse should trust their rider instead.

It was too bad that some of the other riders hadn't spent time training their ponies like I had with Norton.

I was so proud when the judge awarded first place to Norton and me.

"I had no choice," she said. "Norton certainly was the best-behaved pony in the class."

Jillian Jones seemed surprised at our award. But I always knew my Norton was a blue-ribbon pony. Now the whole world knows it too.

It's Showtime!

Pony owners who take part in shows want to impress the judges. One way is to make sure their ponies look ready to compete.

THE DAY BEFORE THE SHOW

It is time for the pony to get clean! A good grooming removes dead skin and dust. Then the owner gives the pony a shampoo and rinse.

Once the pony is clean, it needs a haircut. The owner clips the hair along the pony's jaw, mouth, and nose, inside the ears, and under the horse's face.

Next comes braiding. Braiding the tail and mane keeps the hair from tangling or getting dirty. The braid may be a simple three-part braid or something fancier with ribbons or flowers.

AT THE SHOW

Most of the grooming work is done the day before. But a pony needs a little refreshing when it arrives at the show.

A nice brushing smooths down the pony's coat. Next, the owner checks the pony's feet for stones that need to be removed. Finally, a spray of fly repellent keeps the pesky bugs away.

ABOUT THE AUTHOR

While growing up, Bernadette Kelly desperately wanted her own horse. Although she rode other people's horses, she didn't get one of her own until she was a grown-up. Many years later, she is still obsessed with horses. Luckily, she lives in the country where there is plenty of room for her four-legged friends. When she's not writing or working with her horses, Bernadette takes her two children to pony club competitions.

ABOUT THE ILLUSTRATOR

Liz Alger loves horses so much that she left suburbia to live in the rambling outskirts of Melbourne, Australia. Her new home provides plenty of room to indulge in her passion. Her love of animals, horses in particular, shines through in the delightful and humorous illustrations of Norton, the naughty pony, in the Pony Tales series.

GLOSSARY

GROOM (GROOM)—to brush and clean an animal

HALT (HAWLT)—to stop

INSTINCT (IN-stingkt)—behavior that is natural rather than learned

SADDLE (SAD-uhl)—a seat that goes on a horse

TRAINER (TRAY-nur)—a person who teaches horses to listen to commands

TROT (TROT)—when a horse goes faster than walking but is not quite running

DISCUSSION QUESTIONS

1. Norton didn't seem very excited for his first pony show. Have you ever had to do something you weren't excited about? Discuss your answer.

2. Does Jillian Jones really need advice from Molly? Explain your answer.

3. Do you want to be a horse trainer? Why or why not?

WRITING PROMPTS

1. It was Norton's first time at a pony show. Write about your first time participating in an event.

2. Molly is a little jealous of Jillian Jones. Write a paragraph about a time when you were jealous of someone. How did you handle it?

3. Do you think Molly and Jillian could ever be friends? Make a list of three reasons why they could. Then make a list of three reasons why they couldn't.

TAKE ANOTHER RIDE
WITH NORTON

Norton is a naughty pony. Everyone thinks so.
Well, everyone except his owner, Molly. She thinks
Norton is the most perfect pony in the whole
world, no matter what kind of trouble he causes!

PONY TALES

by Bernadette Kelly

NAUGHTY NORTON

PONY TALES

by Bernadette Kelly

NORTON'S FIRST SHOW